THE BOOGY WOOGY MAN

by

SICILY WILLOWS

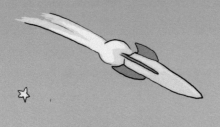

AuthorHouse™
1663 Liberty Drive
Bloomington, IN 47403
www.authorhouse.com
Phone: 1-800-839-8640

Published by AuthorHouse 2/12/2013

ISBN: 978-1-4520-4129-2 (sc)

Library of Congress Control Number: 2012908946

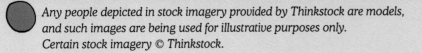

authorHOUSE®

DEDICATIONS

To my children…..I will love you always and forever. You are in every breath I take. You are all special, and each of you unique. I am very blessed to have such wonderful children. All my love….mama.

To my mother…..I hope my children see me in the same light I've always seen you in. You are an amazing woman. Always giving….never taking…. Thank you for all the love and support throughout the years. I know it hasn't always been easy!

To Ms. Sue Ann Payne…..A terrific educator.

Once upon a time, there was a little boy named Henry, and he was very scared of the Boogy Woogy Man that lived under his bed. Every night the Boogy Woogy Man would jump out from under his bed and yell, BOOGY WOOGY, BOOGY WOOGY, BOOGY WOOGY!

"Mommy Mommy, it's the Boogy Woogy Man," Henry screamed very frightened. "Henry stop being so silly. I've already told you, there is no such thing as the Boogy Woogy man," Mommy explained. "But Mommy, it's true, I see him every night." Henry said. "I'm sure it is just your imagination; now go to sleep, baby". Mommy replied in a comforting voice. Henry pulled his spaceman sheets to his nose until he finally drifted away to sleep.

The next day Henry thought about what Mommy said. But he knew that the Boogy Woogy Man was real, it wasn't his imagination, and he was determined to catch him.

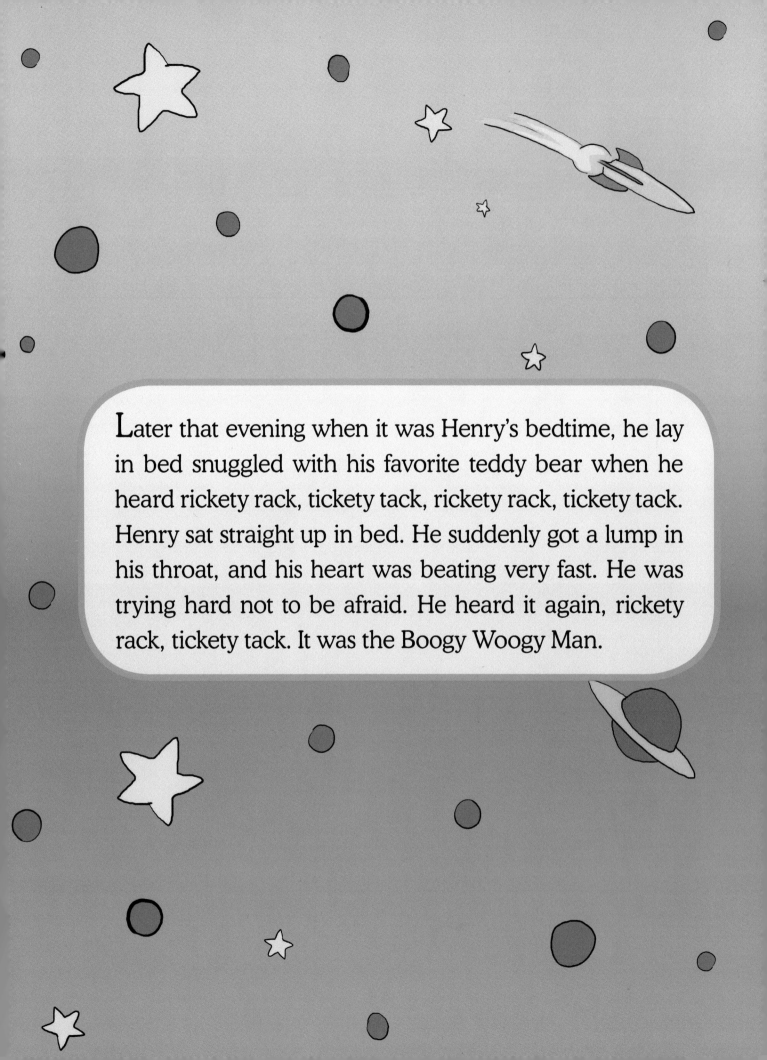

Later that evening when it was Henry's bedtime, he lay in bed snuggled with his favorite teddy bear when he heard rickety rack, tickety tack, rickety rack, tickety tack. Henry sat straight up in bed. He suddenly got a lump in his throat, and his heart was beating very fast. He was trying hard not to be afraid. He heard it again, rickety rack, tickety tack. It was the Boogy Woogy Man.

The Boogy Woogy Man jumped from under his bed. AHHH! BOOGY WOOGY! BOOGY WOOGY! Henry threw the cover over his head, his heart was beating very fast now, and he thought he was going to cry. There was no way he could catch the Boogy Woogy Man; he was just too scared.

Henry lay in bed, hoping the Boogy Woogy Man was gone; he peaked his head from under the cover. The Boogy Woogy Man had disappeared. Henry was still really scared but he also felt bad because he wasn't brave enough to catch the Boogy Woogy Man. How could he catch the Boogy Woogy Man and be scared too? Catching the Boogy Woogy Man would take a lot of courage.

The very next night, Henry lay in his bed knowing the Boogy Woogy Man would try to scare him again. He was determined to capture him.

"BOOGY WOOGY, BOOGY WOOGY, BOOGY WOOGY," the Boogy Woogy Man shrieked. Henry quickly pulled his sheets over his head. "No, I have to be brave," he thought. He peered one eye from under his sheets.

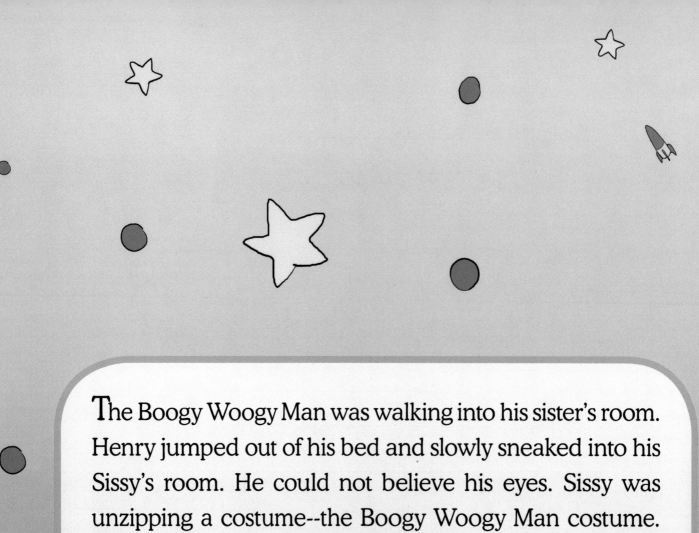

The Boogy Woogy Man was walking into his sister's room. Henry jumped out of his bed and slowly sneaked into his Sissy's room. He could not believe his eyes. Sissy was unzipping a costume--the Boogy Woogy Man costume. She was giggling because she had scared him. It had been Sissy all along.

She had been scaring Henry every night. "Hmm," Henry thought. He knew just the thing to teach Sissy a lesson.

The next night Henry waited until he knew Sissy was sleeping. He snuck very quietly into her room and slipped into the Boogy Woogy Man costume.

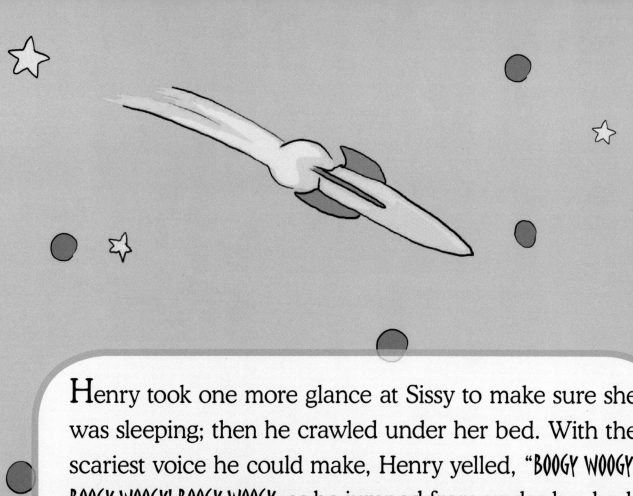

Henry took one more glance at Sissy to make sure she was sleeping; then he crawled under her bed. With the scariest voice he could make, Henry yelled, "BOOGY WOOGY! BOOGY WOOGY! BOOGY WOOGY, as he jumped from under her bed. Sissy awoke so scared her eyes were as big as saucers, and she tumbled onto the floor. Henry couldn't help but laugh. "Henry," she shrilled, "Is that you?" Henry unzipped the costume--still laughing, "I guess you know how it feels for someone to scare you," Henry declared.

"You're right," Sissy confessed, "it's not very nice to scare people--especially little brothers. I'm sorry Henry." Henry and Sissy laughed about the silly Boogy Woogy Man for the rest of the night!

ABOUT THE AUTHOR

She lives in the beautiful country side of Louisiana with her three amazing children and the love of her life, where they take full advantage of the "Sportsman's Paradise." She's always dreamt of becoming a writer so she could inspire readers, and hopefully make them smile. She has always enjoyed using her imagination and writing stories as a small child. One of her favorite memories is sitting under her Aunt Jewel's willow tree--bringing her imagination to life. Her life is blessed with so many things. Her husband and children being the biggest of her blessings. She is a very fortunate woman to have such a wonderful family. She quotes," They are definitley what defines me as an indivisual." Her children inspire her to write her books with thier constant and never ending escapades, while her husband always supports her in all her endeavors.